W9-BRT-029

Dinosaur vs. SCHOOL

BOB SHEA

Disney • Hyperion Books/New York

For information address Disney • Hyperion Books, 125 West End Avenue, New York, New York 10023.

First Edition
10 9 8 7 6 5 4 3 2 1
H106-9333-5-14060
Printed in Malaysia

Reinforced binding

Library of Congress Cataloging-in-Publication Data
Shea, Bob, author, illustrator.—First edition
pages cm
Summary: Fearless Dinosaur takes on new challenges as he starts preschool, from meeting new friends to pasting glitter and googly eyes, but one task requires assistance from everyone.
ISBN 978-1-4231-6087-8
[1. Dinosaurs—Fiction. 2. Nursery schools—Fiction. 3. Schools—Fiction. 4. Humorous stories.] I. Title. II. Title: Dinosaur versus school.
PZ7.S53743D1g 2014
[E]—dc23
2013025784

www.disneyhyperionbooks.com

For Ryan

ROAR!

I'M A DINOSAUR!

ROAR!

I'm going to school!

roar!

roar!

Dinosaur versus . . .

meeting new friends!

ROAR!
ROAR!
7

DINOSAUR
WINS!

Dinosaur versus . . .

dressing up!

ROAR!
Roar! Shoes!
Roar! Hats!

DINOSAUR
ROAR!
ROAR!
ROAR!
DINO
WINS!

Dinosaur versus . . .

glitter, glue, and googly eyes!

ROAR!
SHAKE!
SHAKE!
Roar!
Sprinkle!
Roar!
Glue!
GLUE

Dinosaur wins!

roar!

roar!

roar!

Dinosaur versus . . .

monkey snacks!

ROAR!
Roar, raisins!
Roar, apples!
RAISINS

DINOSAUR
WINS!

roar!

roar!

roar!

Dinosaur versus . . .

making music!

STRUM
STRUM
ROAR!
PLINKA
PLINK
RAT
TAT
TAT
TAT
TAT
toot!
chicca
chicca
chicca
wheeze

DINOSAUR
WINS!
RUM
PA
PUM

Now Dinosaur and his friends will do something they have NEVER done before . . .

CLEAN UP

OH, NO!

It's too much for one dinosaur!

But when everyone helps . . .

EVERYONE
WINS!